Follow the winding stream to the
edge of the jungly forest and meet...

ZIGBY THE ZEBRA
OF MUDWATER CREEK.

Zigby the Zebra loves being outdoors, getting
up to mischief. There are always wonderful
adventures waiting to happen but
sometimes he can't help trotting
straight into trouble!

Meet his friend, the African guinea fowl,
Bertie Bird. He's easily scared and
thinks his friends are far too naughty...but
he'd hate to miss the action!

McMeer is the cheeky meerkat who loves
showing off. His tricks can cause lots of
problems, but he always knows how to have fun!

Zara is Zigby's young cousin. She may only be
little but she usually gets exactly what she wants!

It was the day of the Mudwater Carnival
and Zigby was busy getting ready when
his cousin, Zara, ran in.

ZIGBY™
AND THE MONSTER

BRIAN PATERSON

HarperCollins *Children's Books*

Have you read all the books about Zigby?

Zigby Camps Out
Zigby Hunts for Treasure
Zigby and the Ant Invaders
Zigby Dives In

For younger readers:

Zigby – The Birthday Party
Zigby – The Go-Kart
Zigby – The Picnic
Zigby – The Toy Box

For William, Charles and Henry

First published in paperback in Great Britain by HarperCollins Children's Books in 2005

1 3 5 7 9 10 8 6 4 2
ISBN: 0-00-717423-3

HarperCollins Children's Books is a division of HarperCollins Publishers Ltd.

Text copyright © Brian Paterson and HarperCollins Publishers Ltd 2005
Illustrations copyright © Brian Paterson 2005

ZIGBY™ and the Zigby character logo are trademarks of HarperCollins Publishers Ltd.

Visit our website at: www.harpercollinschildrensbooks.co.uk

Printed and bound in Hong Kong

"Oh, Zigby!" she gasped, "I've just seen a h-h-horrible monster!"

"A monster?" asked Zigby.
"Yes!" wept Zara, "With **six legs**!"
"Let's go and look," said Zigby.
"I might know who that is."

He fetched his swishy stick, and filled a bag with cakes for later.

Zigby led the way to Tiny the Ant's house.
"He's not my monster!" cried Zara.

"*My* monster was **spotty!**"
"Aha," said Zigby.
"I know who *that* is."

The two cousins trotted down
the path to a sunny bank.

Zigby tapped it with his swishy stick.
"Come out, monster!" he said sternly.

A lizard popped out of a hole.
"Ooh!" squeaked Zara.
"That's not *my* monster.

Mine had a **curly tail**."
"Why didn't you say so?" said Zigby.

Further on, they heard chattering in the bright leaves overhead. "That's no monster," sighed Zara. "*My* monster had lots of **sharp, white teeth**."

Zigby led the way past dark mud pools
to the edge of the creek, where something
was wallowing in the water…

"AAGH!! That's not the monster, it's a crocodile," cried Zara. "RUN!" shouted Zigby.

"I don't believe you ever saw a monster," said Zigby crossly. "I *did*," sniffed Zara, "and now I'm fed up and hungry."

"That gives me an idea," said Zigby, unpacking the cakes. "Let's make a trap."

Zigby put out some cakes.
They sat and they waited.
At last, there was a rustling…

...and there was the **scariest** creature Zigby had ever seen! It had **six legs**, spots, **a curly tail** and **sharp, white teeth**.

"Th-th-that's my monster!" Zara cried.

They shivered with fright, as the monster gobbled the cakes. Then it started to bulge and wobble, until…

...out tumbled their friends,
Bertie Bird and McMeer.
"It's you two!" shouted Zigby.
"Do you like our carnival costume?"
giggled McMeer.

Just then Ella the
elephant arrived. "Come on,
everyone!" she said. "We'll be
late for the carnival."

Soon, Zigby and Zara were
riding through Mudwater Creek.
The carnival had begun!

Later, McMeer and Bertie won
a prize for their costume.
They let Zara cuddle it
all the way home.